Samuel French Acting Edition

I0591791

Lila Cante

by Mark Snyder

ⅠSAMUEL FRENCHⅠ

SAMUELFRENCH.COM   SAMUELFRENCH.CO.UK

FOR PRODUCTION ENQUIRIES

UNITED STATES AND CANADA
Info@SamuelFrench.com
1-866-598-8449

UNITED KINGDOM AND EUROPE
Plays@SamuelFrench.co.uk
020-7255-4302

Each title is subject to availability from Samuel French, depending upon
country of performance. Please be aware that *LILA CANTE* may not be
licensed by Samuel French in your territory. Professional and amateur
producers should contact the nearest Samuel French office or licensing
partner to verify availability.

MUSIC USE NOTE

Licensees are solely responsible for obtaining formal written permission from copyright owners to use copyrighted music in the performance of this play and are strongly cautioned to do so. If no such permission is obtained by the licensee, then the licensee must use only original music that the licensee owns and controls. Licensees are solely responsible and liable for all music clearances and shall indemnify the copyright owners of the play(s) and their licensing agent, Samuel French, against any costs, expenses, losses and liabilities arising from the use of music by licensees. Please contact the appropriate music licensing authority in your territory for the rights to any incidental music.

IMPORTANT BILLING AND CREDIT REQUIREMENTS

If you have obtained performance rights to this title, please refer to your licensing agreement for important billing and credit requirements.

LILA CANTE received its world premiere production in October 2009 by At Hand Theatre Company (Dan Horrigan, artistic director; Justin Scribner, producer) in New York City. It was directed by Sara Sahin; the scenic design was by Eli Kaplan-Wildman; the costume design was by Nicole Wee; the lighting design was by Ryan Bauer; the sound design was by Julian Mesri; casting was by Michael Cassara; graphic design was by Jeff Hardy; photography was by Zachary Gross and Joshua Zirschky; the production stage manager was Melissa Magliula; the assistant director was Laura A. Wright; and the managing director was Kim Baillargeon. The cast was as follows:

GREG . . . . .Ryan Spahn

KEITH . . . . .Matt Shofner

NINA . . . . Danielle Di Vecchio

MOLLY . . . . Rebecca Hart

SPECIAL THANKS: Tabi Magar, Jon Levenson, Pete Forrester, Tobi Kanter, Erik Gratton, Megan Carboni, Laura Kenyon, Jackie Freeman, Nick Gaswirth, Carlye Pollack, Robert Moran, Jason Kallus, Jessica Rodriguez, Orange Hanky Productions, OU Playwrights Workshop, Theatre of NOTE, Cydney Rooks, William Nedved, Heather Schmucker, Michael Cassara, Jeremy Fulwiler, Jimmy Groh, Gerald Doherty, Doug McGraw, and the Ohio Five. RIP Brandon Lacy Campos.

CHARACTERS

(in order of appearance)

GREG – 30s, a photographer
KEITH – Early 20s, a young man
NINA – 40s, a music company executive
MOLLY – Late 20s, a musician
THE FANS – A wide spectrum of recorded voices

SETTING

Lower East Side, New York City

TIME

Fall 2005

AUTHOR'S NOTES

Lila Cante is pronounced *Lie-lah Cant (as in "cannot")*

To my mother Mary Alice

ACT ONE

(Interlude: **FANS***.)*

(In the darkness, a collage of sound – music, radio static, voices singing, cheering – fading into the strum of an electric guitar; slowly at first, tunings, then picking up the rhythm of an actual song.)

(A series of recorded interviews with people of all ages, colors, and sexes – music fans – accompanies the music.)

FAN #1. Ten songs.

FAN #2. On cassette. Side A, then you had to turn it over for Side B. Remember those?

FAN #4. Her guitars had all this personality. You could tell who was playing in the first couple of seconds. And the power!

FAN #5. I learned her back-up harmony, which is really textured and tricky.

> *(Light from a static television finds a* **WOMAN** *sitting on the floor, playing the guitar. She begins singing aloud, a wordless voice in the dark.)*

FAN #2. I saw her eight times.

FAN #1. Twice! Her first show on the West Coast.

KEITH. Only once. But it's still the best rock show I've ever seen.

FAN #5. She forced me to break up with my boyfriend.

FAN #2. Dude, she helped me get a boyfriend!

FAN #3. My husband and I walked down the aisle to the title track from her album. Aunt Lucille was mortified.

FAN #4. They lumped her in with the grunge gals, but what she sang about - my niece is into her now.

FAN #3. I stopped listening when I had my first child. Time to grow up. And she didn't seem engaged anymore –

FAN #8. Music today sucks, no wonder she wasn't around anymore.

FAN #1. Nobody else was like her. She knew that, so she didn't try to compete!

FAN #4. She knew that she had done what she came here to do.

KEITH. We won't forget.

FAN #6. Nobody forgets their favorite singer.

FAN #5. And we won't let her go.

> *(The power fueling the TV and the electric amp blows, plunging the* **WOMAN** *into darkness.)*

> *(Lights change.)*

Scene One

(A door opens, revealing **GREG** *and* **KEITH** *kissing against the hallway wall.* **KEITH** *has his leg up around* **GREG**'s *waist;* **GREG**'s *hands are roaming freely down the back of* **KEITH**'s *jeans. There is a package at their feet.)*

GREG. The DJ should be banned from that place.

KEITH. I had fun.

GREG. Guys squeezed into every crevice and he can't keep the music going?

KEITH. We got a chance to talk.

(Kiss.)

In five-second breaths.

GREG. "Nice jeans."

KEITH. They're old.

GREG. "What does your tattoo say?"

KEITH. "It's Latin for 'Lick me here'."

(Kiss.)

We still got to dance. I'm dripping.

GREG. Here –

(Pulls up his shirt to wipe **KEITH**'s *face.)*

Let me.

*(***KEITH*** places his hand on* **GREG**'s *bare chest.)*

KEITH. Your heart's racing, Greg.

GREG. Long day.

KEITH. *(Laughs.)* Goosebumps!

GREG. Your ring –

KEITH. *(Pulls his hand away.)* Oh!

GREG. – It's just a little cold –

KEITH. Sorry –

GREG. – No. Your hand is so soft. Like a vulture's wing.

(Kisses **KEITH**'s *hand.)*

GREG. *(Cont.)* Tonight was real fun.

KEITH. I hope it's not over. Or should I tell you I have to be getting home?

> (**KEITH** *kisses* **GREG**'s *neck;* **GREG** *looks into the apartment: a mattress on the floor in the corner. Dim light.)*

GREG. Do you want to come inside for a little while?

KEITH. I thought that was pretty clear when we split the cab.

> *(Notices the package as he steps inside.)*

Uh-oh.

GREG. What's the matter?

KEITH. *(Picks it up.)* Your boyfriend sent you a present.

GREG. I doubt it.

> *(Takes the package, closes the door.)*

You'll have to excuse the, um – *lack* in here. I'm making some adjustments to the place, clearing the junk away. It turns out that clutter is not my aesthetic.

KEITH. Simple. I like it.

GREG. *(Tosses the package aside.)* I suppose you want some water, or –?

KEITH. Aren't you going to open it?

GREG. Now that is not very hospitable.

KEITH. Ha, but it could be important. Go on. I can wait.

GREG. I guess we're different. I can't.

> *(He kisses* **KEITH**, *pushing him further into the room.)*

KEITH. Did you take that photo?

GREG. Yup.

KEITH. *(Looks around.)* Did you take all these photos?

GREG. Well, nobody else lives here, so –

KEITH. Are they all men?

GREG. Um, mostly. Yeah. Is that odd?

KEITH. No, I just didn't think you were really a photographer.

GREG. I've been taking photos since I was a kid. What did you think I meant? Or weren't you listening?

KEITH. I was, I was –

GREG. Hold still. You have something – on your cheek –

> (**GREG** *grabs* **KEITH** *and licks his cheek, releases him.*)

KEITH. I'm, uh, new in town.

GREG. Shocking.

KEITH. So I don't really know – how exactly – this –

GREG. Relax. You're doing fine. I'm rooting for us.

> *(Pause.)*

KEITH. Um, this photo –

GREG. Don? Yes, that *is* a man.

KEITH. *(Squinting at the photo.)* You can't really tell in that position –

GREG. I was trying to get the burn marks on his forehead to hit the light a certain way, so we could see the color, but he sweat a lot and I got Vaseline on the lens cap. He was a real trooper that night.

KEITH. Intense. In a good way.

GREG. Thanks –

KEITH. Keith.

GREG. You're real sweet to say so, Keith.

> (**KEITH** *kisses him.*)

I've been working a lot, back-to-back-to-back sessions. So tonight, I just wanted to have fun.

KEITH. Have an adventure.

GREG. And here you are.

KEITH. I wanted to get into some mischief too.

GREG. Well, if you keep hanging out in that neighborhood and walking up to guys at the bar –

KEITH. Do you ever take photos of your friends?

GREG. These are mostly visitors. They always want to talk about themselves. They never stay very long, so I can't overthink the photographs. It just happens.

KEITH. Why do they leave?

GREG. They don't like how I see them. Ugh, I sound pretentious.

KEITH. It's hot.

GREG. Like I'm writing my artist's statement for some catalogue at the Whitney.

KEITH. You're hot. I can't believe how many creative people there are roaming around this city.

GREG. And you like that?

KEITH. It's intimidating. I read stuff online about how dreary New York had become for artists, with all these clubs and galleries closing. Real estate tycoons fly over from Europe and buy up all the buildings so they can knock them down. But when I got here and started meeting people? It feels like it's the 80s or something.

GREG. Who have you met?

KEITH. Well, you. Some music people. I used to think, I don't know, that I could be in a band or something.

GREG. Ah, you're a musician.

KEITH. Well I like music a lot.

GREG. Do you play an instrument?

KEITH. Not really –

GREG. *(Touches him.)* You have the lips for a trombone.

KEITH. My brother left his CD collection behind when he moved out. So I listened to all kinds of stuff – Pavement and Missions of Burma, Sonic Youth, Lila Cante, Hole –

GREG. Real "indie" sort of guy?

KEITH. He was always whining about how fucked up the radio got after Kurt Cobain died. He followed my dad out to Arizona. Leaving my mother and me was the boldest move he ever made. And after listening to his music for so long, I see how he was able to do it. I had a soundtrack to play whenever Mom was freaking out about money or when I was bored. Cornfields are not very comforting, but Superchunk was. Music pushed me on the bus to New York, kind of.

>   (**GREG** *kisses him.*)

GREG. Cornfields sound really peaceful, Keith.

KEITH. Have you always lived in New York?

GREG. No.

>   (*Pause.*)

KEITH. So? Where are you from?

GREG. Everywhere.

KEITH. What state is that in?

GREG. Uh, it's just how my family worked out.

KEITH. Well, maybe some of your travels will rub off on me.

>   (**KEITH** *reaches for* **GREG**; **GREG** *takes his fingers and puts them in his mouth. Pause.*)

GREG. You taste like licorice.

KEITH. *(Reaches for him.)* Maybe your boyfriend sent you candy.

GREG. *(Stops him.)* I think it's time for us to say good night, Keith.

KEITH. Why? I'm just teasing.

GREG. I don't have a boyfriend. Okay?

KEITH. You hardly said anything at the club, I just figured –

GREG. You're a cute kid.

KEITH. C'mon! It's your turn!

GREG. We're not taking turns, Keith.

KEITH. *(Looking back at the walls.)* Fine, so where is the picture of you up here?

GREG. *(Points.)* This is me, and that one is me. They're all of me in some way or another. These are what I see when I look at other men, when I look at you. Do you want to go now too?

KEITH. I love that you're even looking, Greg. Take my photo.

GREG. Is that what you want?

KEITH. *(Re a photo.)* I don't know if I'd want to have that metal rod stuffed in my mouth and pulled back with leather straps attached to my ankles like that, but –

GREG. Yeah, Ben wanted to keep the leather.

KEITH. I've been walking around this city for almost a month, and you're the first person to invite me anywhere. If this is where you are headed, then let's go.

GREG. Okay. Sure.

KEITH. Can I take off my shoes?

GREG. Maybe you should see my book before you get cozy.

> *(**KEITH** kicks off his shoes.)*

KEITH. Sure.

GREG. Don't try to climb out the window.

> *(**GREG** exits. **KEITH** makes a beeline for the package by the door, looking at the name on it. He sits on the mattress and undoes two buttons on his shirt. His eyes turn to the ceiling; he stares. **GREG** returns with a glass of water and a large, flat hardcover book.)*

KEITH. *(Averts his eyes.)* You need a chair in here.

GREG. Do you like him?

KEITH. Who?

> *(**GREG** pulls his head back, toward the ceiling, then hands him the book.)*

GREG. The color reproduction is on pages forty-one and forty-two.

KEITH. Is that what you would do with me?

GREG. If you pant hard enough. Isn't he beautiful?

KEITH. I can't see his face. It's dark in here. His body's twisted.

GREG. He started crying into my shoulder when I pulled his leg around my waist. I'm holding him up into the camera lens.

KEITH. Turn on a light.

GREG. *(Points, hovering over* **KEITH**.*)* His face is right there, peering out from under my arm –

> *(The book falls to the floor.)*

KEITH. So dark – there's gook on his face –

GREG. Blood.

KEITH. I can't – turn on the lights!

GREG. That is where we're heading, Keith.

KEITH. C'mon turn up the light!

> *(Lights brighten.* **KEITH** *scrambles for the book, still staring at the ceiling.* **GREG** *begins setting up the camera tripod in the corner of the room.)*

GREG. It's not real.

KEITH. He's not?

GREG. He wanted to look that way. He asked me to show how he feels inside.

> *(***KEITH** *is flipping pages, frantically.)*

KEITH. Tell me, tell me about these.

GREG. Some of those photos were taken when I was eight years old. Early work. Lots of effort on display. This new show is completely off the radar, different.

> *(Re the ceiling.)*

Makes him look like a rough sketch.

KEITH. This cover isn't old.

GREG. That photo was my first.

KEITH. But I've seen it somewhere.

GREG. It's ancient.

KEITH. Those hands clapped together on that very specific rock? Wearing a bracelet.

GREG. Yup.

KEITH. She's not a man.

> *(Pause.)*

GREG. Actually, the bracelet is a hair ribbon, a blue hair ribbon, wrapped around her wrist a few times –

KEITH. And you were eight?

GREG. It was a fluke.

KEITH. We both know where I've seen it.

GREG. This is what I see –

> *(Pours the water from the glass on* **KEITH**.*)*

You're like a wet little puppy, digging his nose in the dirt. Now lay down.

KEITH. It's an album cover.

GREG. What?

KEITH. That photo. I've seen it on a CD. You shot album covers at eight years old?

GREG. Once.

> *(Pause.)*

KEITH. Did you get to meet her?

GREG. Keith.

KEITH. Did you know her?

GREG. The last person I want to talk about is – Please lay down.

KEITH. I'm interested in you.

GREG. I don't matter. Let's focus on you.

KEITH. Okay.

GREG. Relax while I set up.

KEITH. Wait, where are you going?

> *(***GREG*** exits again, taking the glass with him.*
> ***KEITH*** searches, finds the package.* ***GREG*** *returns*
> *quickly with a small box of supplies.)*

GREG. What are you doing?

KEITH. *(Re the address on the package.)* Who do you know in Iowa City?

GREG. I have no idea what that is.

KEITH. *(Shakes it.)* Let's see –

> (GREG *grabs the package away from* KEITH.)

GREG. What are you doing here?

KEITH. I – I – What do you mean?

GREG. You either think I'm really stupid or –

KEITH. I'm just playing around!

GREG. You still want this?

KEITH. YES!

> (GREG *lies down on the mattress with the camera cord.*)

GREG. C'mere.

> (KEITH *moves near* GREG; GREG *pulls* KEITH *into position over him and starts shooting.*)

KEITH. I can't see your face.

GREG. It doesn't work that way.

KEITH. Did you meet Lila Cante? I know it's the cover of Lila Cante's CD.

GREG. Don't move.

> (GREG *changes their position, keeps snapping.*)

KEITH. She came to Missouri to play this outdoor summer festival. She followed Porno for Pyros, and walked out with her guitar, by herself, and just started to play. After maybe thirty seconds, everybody was quiet. Behind me I heard this girl crying.

GREG. Let's try something else.

> (GREG *slides out from under* KEITH, *poses him, continues taking shots.*)

KEITH. Her voice is what stopped everybody, swooping up and down, holding the songs together while her hands seemed to skate over the guitar strings. She got the whole crowd clapping the rhythm during one song while she just threw her head back and laughed –

(GREG has pulled out a razor and starts cutting away KEITH's shirt.)

KEITH. *(Cont.)* Hey! Don't cut –

GREG. *Trust me.* It's gonna be great.

(Yanks the shirt away.)

You won't need it.

(Pause.)

Go on! You want to keep talking about her, keep talking.

KEITH. Uh, she played her whole album in exactly the same order, uh, and she did the extra verse from "Winter Horses" which she last did in Houston 1999 – WHAT ARE YOU DOING?!

GREG. Hold still.

KEITH. Uh, then she did some covers –

GREG. Stop shaking.

(Pulls KEITH's head back, kisses him.)

God you look sexy. Go on, get it out of your system. Tell me about the covers she sang.

KEITH. And, uh, she had her daughter come out and they sang together on one of her daughter's tunes, but her song wasn't as good.

GREG. Now. Take a deep breath.

KEITH. You feel good.

GREG. *(Click.)* Deep breath.

KEITH. Your skin feels nice on mine.

(GREG opens KEITH's pants.)

Touch me, Greg.

(Click. Reaches for GREG's pants)

Let me touch you now.

(GREG stops him, turns him away.)

GREG. The window, look out the window.

KEVIN. I want to look at you.

(GREG *releases* KEITH, *retreats back to the camera case to reload.*)

KEITH. You know, when I saw you at the club, the way you sat at the bar? Your neck was working double-time to make sure your head didn't hit the bar top. You looked like you were living inside of a migraine.

GREG. And you just assume that talking about some old photo that may or may not have been taken for Lila Cante – ?

KEITH. I just want to comfort you.

GREG. *(Points.)* Cameron hung in a sling on a hook behind my bathroom door there for twelve hours. He gave me comfort. Look at him! Jason and Scott over here almost broke their femurs trying to dominate each other while I waited for the exact moment when they were both weak and both wanted to give up – I caught that. I captured them. Bodybuilders crying like little boys. All of this gives me plenty of comfort!

(KEITH *pulls* GREG *into a kiss.*)

Most people – most guys, anyway – don't want to see the truth about themselves. I'm smart, I can't help it. And I show them the truth. They can't wait to walk out the door. Are you going to follow them or me?

(KEITH *pulls his pants off and settles back onto the mattress.*)

KEITH. I like it here.

GREG. Good.

(*Click. Click.*)

I need to see your eyes. Don't close them.

KEITH. Right.

(GREG *cuts some of* KEITH*'s hair.*)

KEITH. *(Cont.)* Are you cutting my hair?!

GREG. This is how I see you.

KEITH. Balding?

GREG. Injured. Lila was injured, you know.

KEITH. She was?

GREG. I mean, that's what you want to hear about, right? Such a big fan.

KEITH. I'm not a fan.

GREG. Bullshit.

KEITH. But she was this huge –

GREG. Think you have her all figured out –

KEITH. – I don't! That's the point! You knew her. Why didn't she write any more songs?

> (**GREG** *reaches behind the mattress.*)

GREG. Well, she's dead.

> (*Binds* **KEITH**'s *mouth with a piece of his shirt.*)

She was my mother.

> (*Pulls* **KEITH** *into position.*)

You'll feel this tomorrow.

> (**KEITH** *gives a muffled cry.* **GREG** *snaps the photo. Blackout.*)

> (*Interlude:* **NINA**.)

> (*Chaos of sound, followed by the squeal of tape on an audio deck. We hear the worn recording of a voice and guitar.*)

> (*A pool of light finds* **NINA**.)

NINA. I first heard her play in a supplies closet. Truth. She shows up with this six-string guitar and I think a kazoo, and this tiny amp, and she pleads and pushes her way in, chases me into the closet and plops down on a stack of old *Spin* magazines, plugs in, throws her head back, and plays! And when she started singing that first song, I realized that this glorified assistant job was going to pay off. See, when the label gobbled up my little indie and put me on the payroll, they wanted both some credibility *and* a bucket of money. A cassette tape full of songs.

> *(A look.)*

Luckily, she ran into a fellow rock chick. A sister. And together we turned those ten songs into cultural history. I wish there were more songs out there.

> *(Behind her,* **GREG** *has opened the package and pulled out a set of cassette tapes, wrapped in rubber bands.)*

> *(The auto deck switches off.)*

> *(Lights change.)*

Scene Two

(The next afternoon.)

*(**MOLLY** stands in the middle of the room, a guitar strapped to her back, studying the photos.)*

MOLLY. *(To herself.)* Busy busy busy.

*(**GREG** enters, carrying a large portfolio sleeve. He stops when he sees **MOLLY**, then closes the door.)*

Not exactly a welcome mat, but I see real accomplishment here. Complexity.

(Sees photograph above her.)

Oh! Hello up there! I'm glad I waited on lunch until I got a look-see at you!

*(Back to **GREG**.)*

Funny, I don't see myself anywhere. Spent all those years with a camera in front of your face, and still pretty much a pussy-free zone. My feelings aren't hurt. Don't worry. In fact, seeing all the bile dripping off these photos, maybe it's a compliment.

GREG. Totally.

MOLLY. Your number doesn't work.

GREG. Cell phone.

MOLLY. You have a cell phone? I take it then you also didn't get the fax. I was in a grocery store trying to send you a fax.

(Pause.)

Hi!

GREG. Hey.

MOLLY. You look good.

GREG. Thanks.

MOLLY. *(Re the photographs.)* I didn't realize you were so athletic.

GREG. You broke in to tell me that?

MOLLY. I have the key.

>   *(Tosses it on the floor.)*

Family apartment, Greg.

GREG. Right.

MOLLY. Though I totally forgot which building. I circled that dog park across the Square looking for that coffee place or the graffiti street lamp – anything – to use as a landmark.

GREG. This whole area got a facelift.

MOLLY. It's definitely prettier.

GREG. Yeah, I barely know where I am.

>   *(Pause.)*

MOLLY. I did try to find you.

GREG. Yeah, I fed your homing pigeons and sent them on their way.

>   *(**GREG** moves to get the key.)*

MOLLY. We saw the write-up on your show in San Diego last year. It sounded exciting.

GREG. An intimate gallery, but –

MOLLY. Ha, that's how I describe the joints we play – *intimate.*

GREG. Right.

MOLLY. But I mean these are really gutsy. I've been spending a lot of time in Middle America lately and no gallery I've been to would touch the agony on display in these particular photographs –

GREG. Well I'm talking to a gallery in Chicago, so maybe that could change –

MOLLY. Neat!

GREG. – The curator loves the photographs, but isn't sure how he would be able to market a whole show –

MOLLY. He sounds smart.

GREG. And I still snag the random print ad campaign every once in a while, so it's not like I don't have stuff going on.

(*Pause.*)

MOLLY. Yes, you'll have to let us know about Chicago.

GREG. Let you know?

MOLLY. We'd come to support you.

GREG. *Support* me?

MOLLY. I'm proud of you.

(**GREG** *holds up his portfolio.*)

GREG. Look, Molly, I have been out at meetings all morning and these kind of need my attention right now.

MOLLY. She had your photos from that last tour framed. I boxed them up for you along with some cameras you left. That first polaroid Lila gave you –

GREG. Right.

MOLLY. Morris can ship them –

GREG. Don't send them here.

MOLLY. (*Looks around.*) There's room.

GREG. The sentimental clutter is safer with you.

(**MOLLY** *holds up his book.*)

MOLLY. She made us call her "Cover Girl" when we saw this.

GREG. Molly.

MOLLY. She kept insisting that a photo of me was on the very next page, just keep turning, next page –

GREG. You don't sit still!

MOLLY. Goats from a farm in Alabama made the book, but no sister.

GREG. You flashed me in front of Lila's guitar grip.

MOLLY. One time!

GREG. Molly, what are you doing here?

MOLLY. I'm passing through town. I got my *own* meetings.

(Pause.)

We can't be alone together for two minutes now, can we?

GREG. I've been awake for two days.

MOLLY. So get some sleep.

GREG. If I close my eyes, I'll just see this stack of photos. This is what it's like when I'm working, okay? Focus and discipline. It's not personal.

MOLLY. Never is.

GREG. And if you're here for some nostalgic trot down memory lane, take that copy of the book with you. You won't find much else.

*(**MOLLY** holds up her fingers.)*

MOLLY. I painted my fingers and toes indigo blue! Do you like it?

GREG. Real cute, Molly.

MOLLY. Greg –!

GREG. What?!

MOLLY. I'm your sister, you asshole. Give me five minutes, huh?

*(**GREG** sighs.)*

My band's getting better. I found a bass player who actually knows what he's doing, and the drummer doesn't even know who Lila Cante is. He's 20.

GREG. How's Morris?

MOLLY. Staying home tending to everything while I'm off gallivanting across the land. We may try to have a baby next year.

GREG. It's not just the nine months, you know.

MOLLY. Yeah, I'd rather not start a long-term dialogue with my uterus right about now. Life's good.

GREG. Me too.

MOLLY. I wondered, when I didn't hear from you for the funeral.

GREG. I was on a shoot in Brussels for a corn chip campaign.

MOLLY. It didn't make the news in Brussels? "Singer dead at –"

GREG. Heart attack's hardly sensational.

MOLLY. Well, the lawyers were there to sit us both down, go over everything in one meeting so there wouldn't be any confusion –

GREG. I spoke to them.

MOLLY. You did?

GREG. Day I got back.

MOLLY. Oh.

GREG. I don't want anything from the estate. I told them that. I thought –

MOLLY. You thought I'd need that clarification.

GREG. I just didn't think it was appropriate for me to dive into your whole – saga – and start making demands.

MOLLY. You don't want *anything*?

GREG. It was a high-paying corn chip.

MOLLY. What an upstanding position to put yourself in, Greg.

GREG. She knew I wasn't going to be any use sorting through her chaos –

MOLLY. Right, because you are the Professional!

GREG. I wasn't there. You knew what to do.

MOLLY. Those lawyers must have thought you were just mature shit.

GREG. I recall being quite charming – Why am I even talking about this with you? I had the conversation, done.

MOLLY. Fine. Sorry to have bothered you.

GREG. No, this doesn't bother me at all. Seeing you doesn't make me feel anything different. I'm exactly the same. Thanks for checking in. It's awesome seeing you.

(Pause.)

Okay?

MOLLY. Sure.

(He exits.)

Can I have my key back? Greg?

(A door slams his answer.)

*(**MOLLY** looks around, searching. She pulls out a piece of blue ribbon and ties it around her wrist. She sits on the floor, pulling the guitar in her lap.)*

*(As **MOLLY** plays, **GREG** re-emerges.)*

GREG. What are you doing?

MOLLY. Acoustics in here still rock.

GREG. I know that music.

MOLLY. She wrote it, Greg. A new song.

(Pause.)

GREG. She knew there were galleries, that people were seeing my work?

MOLLY. She hoped you were happy.

(Continues playing.)

Going into the chorus again. Sing it with me.

GREG. What's the point – ?

MOLLY. It's just a song! Why are you so scared of a silly little song?

GREG. Sounds like a lullaby.

MOLLY. Are you ready? I'll teach you the words –

GREG. I know the words.

MOLLY. So sing with me.

GREG. You have your life now, why are you invading mine?

MOLLY. Greg, I don't blame you for leaving. You're lucky you got away when you did.

GREG. So let me stay away.

*(**MOLLY** sets the guitar down.)*

MOLLY. I can't do that this time. Sorry.

GREG. You play just like her.

MOLLY. I'm slightly good, huh?

GREG. I don't know the technical details, but –

MOLLY. I wanted to see you, to be able to touch you. She's dead, Greg.

GREG. Nice ribbon.

MOLLY. Fine.

> *(Yanks off the ribbon, all business now.)*

Did you listen to the tapes?

GREG. Tapes?

MOLLY. That package from Iowa City.

GREG. I didn't get a package.

MOLLY. Greg, I had Morris send you cassettes of her demos.

GREG. What demos?

MOLLY. She had this stack of old tunes that she was rewriting and working into new songs. We recorded a whole bunch of stuff together last summer. You just haven't opened it yet. Where does your mail go?

> *(**MOLLY** pushes the guitar into **GREG**'s hands.)*

GREG. I don't know what to tell you.

MOLLY. Well, where are they?

GREG. Jeez, Molly! What's the big deal?

MOLLY. *(Pulls out her phone.)* I need Morris. I'll be right back –

GREG. Molly, what's going on?

MOLLY. Don't fucking move!

> *(She dashes out with her phone.)*

> *(**GREG** takes the guitar and, with great difficulty, finds a chord. He switches chords again, then again. Tries to do it with quick succession, but it doesn't really work. For the first time, **GREG** is awkward.)*

(**MOLLY** *watches him.*)

What are you doing?

(**GREG** *immediately puts down the guitar.*)

GREG. Nothing.

MOLLY. I'm the musician, Greg. Not you –

GREG. Right.

MOLLY. Not you.

(*Takes back the guitar.*)

Morris has the tracking number for the package. It was delivered yesterday. Where is it?

GREG. What's the big deal about some cassettes?

MOLLY. Nina called me.

GREG. Nina – ?

MOLLY. Blunt hair, big watches, Veruca Salt tattoo.

GREG. Eww.

MOLLY. She's now the senior vice president of flim-flam at the label.

GREG. No! No no no no NO!

MOLLY. Greg! Listen!

GREG. You could have handled this with her over email. Why are you pulling me into it?

MOLLY. Did you listen to the lawyers? Because you apparently talk to everybody in the fucking world but ME!

(*A moment.*)

Nina wants to re-release Lila's album for the 20th Anniversary and tack on some extra tracks she found. And according to the lawyers, since we're both executors, one of us has to sign off on the release.

GREG. You are unbelievable.

MOLLY. Lila wanted people to hear the new songs! That's why I sent them to you –!

GREG. So put those songs on with the album.

MOLLY. Nina found these crackling hissing demos Lila made on a bus somewhere in the middle of Lollapalooza. Lila would freak if she heard those now.

GREG. I think you should just let that label do what they want, they will anyway! Sign whatever you need to sign, and be finished with it. You have your own life to worry about, your own band!

MOLLY. But but but – Greg! – She was proud of these songs, on those tapes, she knew they were good. She wasn't all apologies about them. We were up at the house in Shandanken, sitting on these rocks with her cassette recorder, the songs and us.

GREG. Two crazy peas in a pod.

MOLLY. You have to listen to them. Do you know how many fans are crazy to hear new songs from Lila Cante – *anything* new?

GREG. Please don't talk about her crazy fans.

MOLLY. She left that house a mess in taxes. There's debt. It would help me pay for stuff. That's all I'm saying.

> *(Pause.)*

GREG. Whenever I would try calling up there, she always sounded so distracted. I knew it wasn't me – more like the act of picking up the phone like a normal person was really depressing for her. She never wanted to talk about the next tour or who was licensing which song this week. She just wanted to hear about me. And New York. Who I'd run into from the old days. I guess I stopped asking how she was doing. What happened up there?

MOLLY. She was making fires all the time in the living room, chopping up lawn furniture and the kitchen table at one point, to burn for firewood. She couldn't get warm, she kept telling me, and she didn't want to sing when it was cold.

GREG. And you just left her alone like that?

MOLLY. Once we recorded those songs, I didn't have a purpose. She handed me those cassette tapes and told me to go. Plus, I had rehearsals with my own band. She liked being alone. We make choices, Greg. I'm playing to tiny clubs around the block from the arenas Lila would fill.

GREG. How can you keep playing her music?

MOLLY. The songs were a better parent than she was. Those tapes.

GREG. Right.

MOLLY. If you didn't sign for them –

GREG. I didn't.

MOLLY. – Then I have to find that package –

GREG. Of course, that's why you came here.

MOLLY. *(Hesitates.)* I'm happy you're okay.

GREG. Good luck.

MOLLY. When you hear those songs, you'll understand what Lila was trying to do –

GREG. Molly, she's been gone a really long time –

MOLLY. I knew they'd be safe with you.

GREG. – And listening to some cassettes of you two howling into a microphone is not going to bring her back.

MOLLY. You underestimate her. And me.

> *(**MOLLY** exits.)*
>
> *(**GREG** pulls out the tapes, opens one of the cases, and pulls out the cassette. Looking at it, he begins pulling the tape out, strand upon strand.)*
>
> *(After a moment, he pulls out a photograph pencil and starts rewinding the tape slowly back into the cassette.)*
>
> *(Lights change.)*
>
> *(Interlude: **KEITH**.)*
>
> *(A remixed version of the original song, with a propulsive beat added to it, making it brighter and more alive.)*

(A pool of light finds **KEITH**.*)*

KEITH. She had been playing for nearly two hours and I cannot take my eyes off her hands: they are taped-up with pieces of metal, like claws, and they move so fast, like a blur of light. I feel like we're having our own conversation, and she's telling me all her secrets. There are secrets sprinkled through her CD. Listen real close and you can hear them. So she's singing "Winter Horses," the last song on the CD, and still playing, she starts over toward our side of the stage. Lila – get this! She touches my head with her hand! I nearly fainted.

(Pause.)

When I grabbed her hand, it was soft and cool like a piece of dry ice. I was lifted out from that sweaty mess of people in the crowd and into her song, like she wrote it for me. I was a part of it.

(Lights change.)

Scene Three

*(Later that evening. The new photos of **KEITH** are
pinned to the wall in a corner, near the stack of
tapes.)*

*(**GREG** is watching **NINA** squint her eyes at the
photographs in front of her and around the room.)*

NINA. Talent is coursing through this room, Greg. Feel it?
Your photos crackle with energy. Do you ever get used
to that sensation? I bet not. My art world friends told
me to race down here and see Lila's son's provocative
work. You know I want to support your family in any
way I can. Even if hanging out in unfinished loft spaces
with cheap lighting fixtures is not exactly in my bag of
tricks.

(Looks to him.)

I assume you've sold them all?

GREG. Not yet.

NINA. Well each one of these is practically leaping off the
wall and climbing into my checkbook!

GREG. I'm working on a new show.

NINA. Music folk get accused of being isolated and aloof,
particularly now with all these labels acting like they're
on the stock market, but I'm plugged into all kinds of
sockets. I saw the billboard for the shoe line you did.
And a couple of those print ads are really dynamic,
Greg. I saved the magazines.

GREG. Do you want me to autograph them for you?

NINA. But these will send your heat index through the
roof!

GREG. I just do the work.

NINA. You're like your mother that way.

GREG. I mean, I can't really afford to say no when an
opportunity falls into my lap, but I try to maintain a
balance –

NINA. Well this is a whole other level, so get that lap ready, kiddo!

GREG. Do you really think so?

NINA. Lila's death has been a blessing in disguise, hasn't it?

GREG. I'm not quite sure what you mean.

NINA. I manage a guy in this band whose girlfriend threw herself out a dorm room window, and he's been writing the most achingly beautiful love songs about her while high as a chandelier.

GREG. Lucky girl.

NINA. Sorrow can lead to tremendous productivity. Some of these images are so full of pain –

GREG. How did you find me?

> (**NINA** *pulls out a ring of keys from her bag, shakes them.*)

NINA. We've paid the rent on this place for almost ten years. She kept trying to hide upstate, avoiding writing songs for that second damn record. We wanted her in the city, getting some grime under her nails.

GREG. It was empty when I moved in.

NINA. You painted that yellow color in the bathroom when you were seven.

GREG. I'll take over the lease.

NINA. Exactly. You should be here. Let's work out the details.

> (*Pulls a bottle of champagne from her bag.*)

I thought we should toast your mama here, together.

GREG. Isn't that a little inappropriate?

NINA. Oh that funeral was full of the past, half-deaf roadies who didn't know when to stand up or sit down. I feel like this a more Lila-esque send-off. Will you join me, Greg?

GREG. You were her boss.

NINA. I was her friend.

GREG. You'd take the train up to the house in Shandanken with a new scheme to bribe her into making another album. You had Smashing Pumpkins make her a Christmas tape.

NINA. They were having their Moment.

GREG. She always had to sign something when you'd show up.

NINA. Lila confided in me. I knew more about her than you might think. That soggy tribute on the Grammys was a joke. She'd want me to celebrate with her son. You know, I admire your guts, Greg. I do. Chaos follows you, little whispers and innuendos about your models. Some make claims against you when they realize what you forced them to do. You're still here doing the work like you said. Lila backstroked in the chaos, didn't she?

GREG. She wasn't bored.

NINA. I like that you don't get caught.

(Hands him the bottle.)

Glasses.

(She exits into the kitchen. **GREG** *picks up the tapes, hesitating what to do with them.)*

GREG. My work flirts with acceptability and boundaries. Every single person's reaction is part of the experience. Critics forget that the viewing audience is always part of my equation and it doesn't work when you view them by yourself.

NINA. *(Offstage.)* And that attitude doesn't frighten off donors?

GREG. Why do you think I'm still taking magazine work.

NINA. *(Offstage.)* We can also talk about that.

*(***GREG*** *hides the tapes.* ***NINA*** *enters with two plastic cups.)*

GREG. What *else* is there to talk about?

NINA. Open the champagne, Greg.

(GREG takes the bottle, opens it with a pop, and pours.)

GREG. I'm shocked you know so much about me.

NINA. Google helps. Do you know that when you type the letter L into the search bar on Google, Lila's name is the second phrase it prompts you? She's got to be googled thousands of times a day to be the second prompt – she beats out Lil Wayne! Do you know what the first prompt is?

GREG. Love?

NINA. "Limewire."

GREG. Lila's idea of technology was a new cassette recorder.

NINA. Yeah, I never got that, why she didn't appreciate digital faster.

(Holds up her glass.)

We will always keep you with us, Lila. Your relevance proves that the best music and the purest of voices outlast every decade and trend. With your bold son's support, I promise to keep that music, your legacy, alive exactly as I know you would want it to be.

(Toasts.)

To Lila. And to us.

GREG. And Molly.

NINA. Yes. And Molly.

(Drinks.)

My assistant has your book.

GREG. You bought my book?

NINA. I gave it out as my Christmas gift. I'm trying to impress you, Greg.

GREG. Why should you care what I think?

NINA. We need to talk about the new Lila Cante project.

GREG. This is a Molly conversation, Nina.

NINA. I'm here to talk to you.

GREG. She didn't want to make another album.

NINA. Oh, the label knew years ago that we weren't going to get another Lila Cante album. So we chose to focus on what we do have. Her album was released once on CD, in a basic analog to digital transfer. We rushed to put it out, so the sound quality is really terrible. So we've put up the cash and gone back to the masters and cleaned up the disc for a better, remastered version of the original album.

GREG. Molly knows this jargon.

NINA. It's stunning. They were able to bring Lila's voice closer to the front of the mix, so we can hear how clear and sharp her harmonies are for the lead vocals. Those musicians sound like they are actually in the same room with her, instead of playing down in the stairwell like they did. Her fan blogs are already buzzing over the possibility of this. *Entertainment Weekly* did this article about the "Top 20 Albums We Wish They'd Re-release" and our album was number one!

GREG. At last.

NINA. Oh there's more. I dug around the vaults and came across some of the alternate tracks she recorded when she was making the album, after she signed with the label. It's just her guitar and another voice doing the harmony. We're including three of those alternate tracks on the new release of this album, a condolence gift for the fans. I find all this very cool.

GREG. Those are solid reasons to release the album again.

NINA. Excellent.

GREG. But Molly –

NINA. Yes, Molly.

GREG. She has her own set of demos.

NINA. Excuse me?

GREG. New songs. If you're going to release stuff –

NINA. Lila didn't write new songs. She sent me everything she recorded, even it if was off some soundboard at a show. Threw cassettes into a box, to my office.

GREG. She wrote them with Molly.

NINA. Were these new songs labeled with the date and a little guitar girl sketched in purple marker?

GREG. I-I-don't know.

NINA. Wait. Do these new songs have titles?

GREG. Why would I know any of that? Molly –

NINA. So you haven't seen any tapes at all?

GREG. I'm only repeating what Molly –

NINA. So *Molly* is the only person besides Lila who knows about these new recordings, these new songs?

GREG. Uh –

NINA. And Molly's singing on these, right? Supposedly with Lila, right?

GREG. Right. Yes.

NINA. You see how it is.

GREG. If her album's still so great why don't you just release the remastered version as is, just the ten songs? Why do you need to mess with it?

NINA. Fans crave context at this stage of their lives. Kim Deal from the Breeders and Suzanne Vega are writing new liner notes.

GREG. You've thought of everything.

NINA. We need you on board. Three demos from 1989.

GREG. Lila wouldn't have written new songs if she didn't want to share them.

NINA. Lila's dead. She doesn't get to decide anymore. You are the grown-up here, Greg. Decide.

GREG. No. NO. This, this, this –

(Shows her a photo of **KEITH.** *)*

– is what I do. This is me. Why did you come down here, Nina? Don't try to invite me where I don't belong.

NINA. Look how straight your teeth are. One of your mother's advances must be in your mouth.

GREG. I'm sorry, Nina.

NINA. You owe us. Your family – Lila owed us – you're the next best – so you owe us.

GREG. Talk to Molly. Please.

NINA. Dealing with your sister's always so traumatic. I wish you got that. And I need one of you.

GREG. You expect us to be these proud torchbearers for her. And we're not. She wanted us to do our own thing. I'm a photographer trying to build a career separate from hers.

NINA. *(Touches the photo of* KEITH.*)* Right. Your career.

GREG. Can't that be enough?

NINA. *(Re the photo.)* He's so torn between showing his fear and enjoying what you're doing to him. Compelling. Do you know his name when you ask him here?

GREG. Keith.

NINA. Look, I can just see his eyes welling up.

GREG. He cried.

NINA. Did you comfort him?

GREG. Of course.

NINA. Good. He looks so alone here.

　　　　　(Studies another.)

Wow, he's going to rip in half here and he's laughing. I like how his head is thrown back with such abandon. I could never be like that. Certainly not in a photograph for all the world to see.

GREG. I'll hold it for you.

NINA. Tempting.

GREG. He's going to be the center of my new show.

NINA. Well. He's stunning.

GREG. He sure is.

NINA. Keith's also fifteen. Loves music and fame.

GREG. Fame?

NINA. From Missouri. Very devoted. Out of all the fans I chatted with online, dangling an opportunity to help release Lila's music back out into the world, he was the first one to buy himself a bus ticket. He doesn't sit in front of his computer all day or hide behind a camera. He makes shit happen. And these photos, what you two did together, these are some major shit.

(Pause.)

Negatives from your print shop are being messengered over to my office right now.

GREG. He consented.

NINA. It takes a phone call to his parents. With the *Daily Post* on the other line.

GREG. You set me up.

NINA. The label really wants to build the fall release schedule around Lila's album, so there was urgency here. I hope you understand. Hell, I think we can pony up some money for this show of yours, even. I'd love to make you a must-see.

GREG. I don't want your money.

NINA. I wouldn't either. It comes with strings.

(Holds up the photos.)

But the fact you seduced and exploited a child?

GREG. He's not – I didn't exploit him.

NINA. That attention would severely cloud our re-release of the album with our three demo tracks.

GREG. And it all snakes back to Lila.

NINA. He did stay the night. I didn't ask him to do that part.

GREG. I am so stupid.

NINA. No you're ambitious, Greg. And smart. That's what makes this so much fun.

GREG. Molly is depending on me, she –

NINA. Do you hear yourself? Molly is the chaos now. More of Lila's nonsense that you don't want to deal with anyway. So don't. Are you going to let her distract you again?

(Pause.)

GREG. Molly can't know.

NINA. Well, she might figure it out –

GREG. Just make him – make *her* – go away. Please.

NINA. No worries. I'll handle Keith. But you're still Lila Cante's son, Greg. She's never going away.

(blackout)

End of Act One

ACT TWO

(Interlude: **GREG**.*)*

(Two clear and vibrant voices singing to a soft acoustic guitar, full of harmonious beauty.)

*(***GREG*** enters an empty space and begins adjusting the lights throughout. Several flat packages, the framed photographs, lean against the wall.)*

GREG. Her guitar got in the way. Everything else took a back seat to this solid piece of wood with strings and a capo clipped on the neck. We learned words like "tuning" and "octaves" along with "apple" and "hello." Molly's first word was "chord." She wrote on this tree stump in the garden, and I hid among the tomato plants, trying to figure her out. What she wrote didn't sound like much, bursts of jumbled notes and words that didn't make any sense. But then she'd take a deep breath and WHOOSH! The whole song came together. I could see what she was singing out behind my eye. So clear. Precise. I got it.

(Hangs the final photograph in the center of the gallery: **KEITH**, *staring directly into the camera lens.)*

Nothing was missing. This *was* her life.

(Lights change.)

Scene One

(The gallery is dim and empty. There is a pounding on the door outside.)

*(**MOLLY** enters with her guitar. She crosses over to the photograph of **KEITH** mounted on the wall.)*

*(**GREG** enters.)*

GREG. Aren't you a little far uptown?

*(**MOLLY** pulls out a razor blade. **GREG** throws down his satchel, grabs her.)*

MOLLY. Get your hands off me.

GREG. I'm not gonna let you make another Molly mess.

MOLLY. LET GO OF ME!

*(**GREG** holds up the razor.)*

GREG. You'd ruin my work?

MOLLY. Right, you're the real artist in this family.

GREG. We open the doors for the guests in 30 minutes. Come back then.

MOLLY. What a fucking joke. Should I just stay outside and watch from the window?

GREG. Bitter Little Sister is beneath you, Molly.

MOLLY. You sold me out. I had to read about it in *Billboard.*

GREG. What was I supposed to do? He's fifteen and she planted him here –

MOLLY. She bribed you with money from the label. Look at this place! You're a corporate puppet, just like Nina. What happened to our pact to stay independent from all this bullshit?

GREG. There can't be independence from the mainstream when there's no mainstream.

MOLLY. You didn't earn this and we both know it.

*(**MOLLY** tries for the photograph again.)*

GREG. Nina knew a guy and got me the gallery, okay?

MOLLY. Ah the prestige. I guess the roaches in the stairwell are wearing skinny jeans too.

GREG. The assistant will escort you out of here. Wait until you see her claws –

MOLLY. I'm not on the walls or on the guest list. Do I even exist in your life, Greg? Does Lila?

GREG. You're not staying here if you're going to be crazy.

> (**MOLLY** *yanks the photograph from the wall. She and* **GREG** *struggle over it.*)

Let go of him.

MOLLY. "Him"? Ha!

> (**GREG** *takes it back.*)

GREG. I don't mess with your songs.

MOLLY. You've never seen me play with my band, what would you know about my songs?

GREG. I've tried –

MOLLY. I'm on the road nearly eight months, four times in New York already this year. You never show up.

GREG. Maybe I was on assignment, I don't know.

MOLLY. Or maybe you're hiding in the dark room of that shell of our old apartment they own. Did you listen to the tapes yet?

GREG. I told you –

MOLLY. They were delivered to you, Greg. I know they were.

GREG. Well, my show has kept me very busy –

MOLLY. This is the life you cut us off for? Dirty pictures? Going home alone and staring at them?

GREG. Lila knew what I was trying to accomplish. She got it.

MOLLY. She pushed me away too. You're just like her.

GREG. I wanted to learn that song of yours when you came to the apartment, I asked you –

MOLLY. LILA's song, not mine. My stuff sounds nothing like her.

GREG. That might be your problem.

MOLLY. So you avoid those tapes because I'm singing on them with Lila? Are you jealous?

GREG. I never got those tapes, I keep telling you –

MOLLY. Quit lying to me!

GREG. Maybe Morris –

MOLLY. Morris did send them. You are lying!

GREG. Maybe he had other plans.

MOLLY. Like what?

GREG. Offers.

MOLLY. Offers?

GREG. Bloggers pay for music they can offer up exclusively on their site. Increases the click-per-link ratio.

MOLLY. Nina's brainwashing you.

GREG. You don't think there was a "Lila Cante Factor" when he met you?

MOLLY. Morris is not like that.

GREG. How do you know?

MOLLY. He grew up listening to Waylon Jennings.

GREG. But he must have known –

MOLLY. He knows who I am, and he's not a starfucker. Sorry.

　　　　　(Pause.)

That kid said he saw a box.

GREG. Keith?

MOLLY. Your fifteen-year-old. Nina must know you have them too.

GREG. When did you talk to Keith? Were you in on this? Were you?

MOLLY. No. He popped up at my show last week, begging me to play him any of her songs. He just wanted to hear one live again. Treated me like a Lila Cante jukebox.

GREG. You let him backstage?

MOLLY. The alley next to the bar was backstage.

GREG. He didn't say anything?

MOLLY. Didn't you do enough damage to his psyche when you took his photo?

GREG. I guess he's gone.

(**GREG** *carefully remounts the photograph of* **KEITH** *on the wall.*)

MOLLY. Isn't that what you wanted?

GREG. Mostly. I let them go as soon as they walk out the door. But he's the centerpiece of my whole show.

MOLLY. That's one way to hold on to him.

GREG. Hopefully by the end of tonight, he'll belong to someone else. Someone who pays cash.

MOLLY. Aren't you curious what she put on those tapes? Don't you want to hear how she sounded after all these years? What she was writing about, thinking about? She talks a lot between the songs, and it's all on there. She was downright chatty that day.

GREG. I don't. Sorry. I'm looking forward. So should you.

MOLLY. Being aloof makes it easy for you. Keeps life so clean.

GREG. Doors close when someone dies. We'll never be able to go back, Molly. Why try?

MOLLY. You try writing songs with that voice in your head, how many get thrown away when you realize you're copying.

GREG. No one is begging you to write songs.

MOLLY. Right and photos of naked guys are real pioneering work?

GREG. There are two hundred clothed people tonight who seem quite excited by them. And I'm not aloof. I'm right where I need to be.

MOLLY. She died six months ago, Greg. And all this noise and attention fell on top of me. Men just show up at the house, claiming she wrote "Winter Horses" about them. Morris moved us to Iowa City to escape. Man, it's so normal there. We eat yellow squash and make soup with kale in it.

GREG. I don't know Iowa, sorry –

MOLLY. That's why I'm telling you about it, you asshole! I sit on his family's front porch and I play the songs we grew up with, hoping a line or a chord change will trigger me. I want to fall into a sobbing mess, heave her fame out of me so I can remember my mom, but it won't happen.

GREG. Crying's overrated anyway.

MOLLY. Thanks for the sympathetic shoulder.

GREG. She belongs to those crazies that build shrines to her online. She belongs to Keith more than to me. Or you. I don't see the point in mourning the idea of someone more than the actual person. Let her fans mourn Lila Cante.

MOLLY. But we need the catharsis, you and me.

GREG. I'm fine, Molly. A critic from *Artforum* is coming tonight and I have a profile in the *Times* on Thursday. And no one is going to ask me about her. I'm someone else now.

MOLLY. People will hear these new songs if I have to release them myself.

GREG. Maybe your band can upgrade to an actual tour bus.

MOLLY. It has nothing to do with my band.

GREG. Catharsis.

MOLLY. We do just fine, thank you.

GREG. But you grew up jamming with Big Audio Dynamite and Midnight Oil, while their girlfriends were in the bathroom peeing on my Jeanne Dunning photographs. I sat in the corner. I earned whatever Nina may or may not be offering me years ago.

MOLLY. This is so wrong, you are so wrong.

GREG. It must be quite different jamming with farmers now. Take those demos and negotiate a big deal for yourself. Be ambitious. Don't hide them behind Lila Cante. She didn't write those songs so I would listen to them.

MOLLY. You don't know that.

GREG. She told me anything essential on the phone.

MOLLY. Really.

GREG. Sure.

MOLLY. You spoke to her.

GREG. I called her. She always picked up.

MOLLY. Always?

GREG. Are you jealous of that too?

MOLLY. You did call once. I saw her look at the ID on the phone and turn away. Speaking to you was apparently a distraction she didn't want to deal with.

GREG. She always picked up.

MOLLY. Instead, she unplugged the phone.

GREG. I'm not surprised.

MOLLY. She died that day.

GREG. You weren't there.

MOLLY. I was.

GREG. But you told me –

MOLLY. Morris took a bike into town, to pick up some groceries, and Lila sat me down with those songs written in her notebook. She had some shows booked and I thought we were going to run through some new arrangements, so she could practice the old stuff. But they were these new songs. And she was determined to get them down on tape right then. We hauled that old cassette player and sat in the garden and made that music. You called –

GREG. I don't want to hear anymore.

MOLLY. But she was too focused, angry that you were interrupting.

GREG. Stop.

MOLLY. On the tape, she talks about you and calling you back. But then she was gone –

GREG. DON'T – Just – don't –!

MOLLY. She was restless and eager and – how happy she sounded about the songs. A new album. Making plans to come out and celebrate with us in Iowa City, cooking with Morris. Like a normal family. And then –

(*Closes her eyes.*)

I've been holding on to this. Wondering what I was going to do with it. And since you're so strong and detached and successful, you should have no trouble carrying the truth around for a while.

GREG. What truth?

MOLLY. She finished her songs, her life's work, put them on tape, handed them to me, and went inside.

(*Pause.*)

Morris found her hanging on a pipe in the hall closet upstairs, from the white leather belt she bought in New Orleans. Some of the beads broke off and fell on the floor.

GREG. You are so sad, Molly.

MOLLY. No, the doctor up in that little village is sad, sad and scared. Apparently, he was writing prescriptions like they were autographs.

GREG. You, but you just – she was *happy* –!

MOLLY. And relieved. Her work was finished. The label gets their album and she gets the last word. It's almost noble, if you think about it. An act of honor. A salute. I mean, aren't we supposed to understand our parents better as we get older, isn't that part of growing up? She yanked that opportunity away. Hanging on a pipe. Out of here.

(*Pause.*)

MOLLY. (*Cont.*) Let's see how you do knowing that.

GREG. I can't –

MOLLY. Sure you can. You're so tough.

GREG. I don't want this, I don't –

MOLLY. I'm glad I listened to Morris. He told me to tell you.

GREG. Glad? Our mother killed herself!

MOLLY. Not our mother, Greg. Lila Cante. It's easier to mourn the idea of a person, right?

> *(Pause.)*

Why wouldn't you listen to those tapes? It's all there.

GREG. Molly –

> *(Finally, a cry.)*

Don't leave me alone!

MOLLY. Two hundred people, your fans. You won't be alone.

> *(Holds out guitar.)*

You want this one? It was Lila's.

> **(GREG** *turns away. She sets the guitar on the floor.)*

GREG. This isn't her show. It's mine. I don't want her here in the corner. I don't want her here at all. She's –

> *(Turns;* **MOLLY** *is gone.)*

Everywhere.

> **(GREG** *digs into his satchel, pulling out the tapes and staring at them. Suddenly he collapses on the ground with the tapes, hitting them with his bag. All poise and attitude have vanished. He is throwing a tantrum.)*

> *(There is a knock behind him at the gallery door.)*

> **(GREG** *tries to collect himself, goes to the wall and pushes two buttons. Hip music starts to play over the speakers; light floods the gallery, with a particular spot focused on the photograph of* **KEITH**.*)*

(Another knock.)

(GREG *sees the guitar. He picks it up and pulls a blue ribbon from inside. He wraps it around his wrist.)*

(blackout)

Scene Two

(Late that night. Lights are down, music's off. The party's over. **GREG** *sits in the middle of the room, tossing business cards on the floor from a stack in his hand, a wine glass at his feet.)*

*(***KEITH** *enters with a backpack.)*

KEITH. I saw you through the window.

GREG. You're late. Even the hired scenesters went home. You missed your big moment.

KEITH. Do all of those people want to buy your photographs?

GREG. Apparently, "The degrading of masculinity in all its shapes and perceived forms finds new life and even a profound dignity in the new work of a photographic sorcerer."

KEITH. Wow.

GREG. A tipsy critic slobbered a sneak peek of his review.

KEITH. Um, so I'm waiting tables in this café? Some man left me this under his check.

(He holds up a postcard from the show.)

GREG. Ah.

KEITH. I couldn't believe it.

GREG. Believe it.

KEITH. I thought you forgot about me after that night.

GREG. It was morning when you left.

(Pause.)

The postcard wasn't my decision. I gave the gallery a stack and they picked.

*(***KEITH** *surveys the room.)*

KEITH. Art patrons are sloppy.

GREG. Prefer music executives?

KEITH. Look, she made it sound like there was all this unreleased material of Lila's and that it was my duty

– I was so bored living at home, nothing was happening there.

GREG. And now you're a poster boy in New York City. You've arrived.

KEITH. She lied to me too, you know.

GREG. *(Drains his wine glass.)* I need to meet some people, Keith.

KEITH. Once she had the negatives of our photos, she stopped calling me. Her emails bounced back. I was subletting a room in this apartment for models she set up and they threw me out when I couldn't pay. She was just gone.

GREG. And you didn't call me.

KEITH. I thought –

GREG. You made me dance with you, practically begged me to take your photos, you spent the night with me –

KEITH. I wanted you.

GREG. Then you corner my sister at her show? You didn't want me that bad.

KEITH. She knew Lila's music and I was scared.

GREG. Can I just let tonight sink in a little bit? I mean, before we start up again about how important my mother was during your crummy queer boy childhood? Would that be so wrong?

KEITH. Better to be a queer boy who goes after what he wants than a guy who hides behind his camera.

GREG. *(Laughs.)* You're pretty tough for fifteen.

KEITH. Fifteen? She told you I was fifteen?

GREG. You are fifteen.

KEITH. Twenty.

GREG. And your parents –

KEITH. I told you the truth about my family. My father and brother left, my mom went berserk. I didn't lie to you about them. She really told you I was fifteen?

GREG. I guess I panicked.

KEITH. *You* panicked?

GREG. Because I was –

KEITH. Scared?

GREG. Cynical. That night was a fluke.

KEITH. It felt real to me in the morning.

GREG. It was real. I have the proof.

> *(Flips the light on, illuminating* **KEITH**'s *photograph.)*

You sold tonight for $8,000. It's being shipped to Minneapolis at the end of the show.

KEITH. You saw me.

GREG. I had to share what I saw in you, what you showed me that night. You looked me straight in the eye and wouldn't let me go. I couldn't just observe you. I had to participate. There are all these colors inside of you, Keith. Don't waste your time on Lila's music.

KEITH. Greg, about Nina.

GREG. *(Grabs him.)* She is the least interesting thing about you right now.

KEITH. I don't want you to be mad at me.

GREG. I'm gonna suck you off in front of your photograph.

KEITH. Oh.

> *(***GREG*** kisses him.)*

When we were dancing together?

GREG. *(Opens* **KEITH**'s *pants.)* Shhh.

KEITH. And Lila's song came on, the remix? I wasn't sure what you'd do. Then you lifted me into the air, singing along with every other man on that dance floor. You looked so happy.

GREG. I was drunk.

KEITH. Proud of Lila.

GREG. *(Rough.)* Stop talking about her. Please.

KEITH. I'm trying to like you, Greg. Give me a little credit. Let me like you.

GREG. There have been plenty of other fans before you, Keith.

KEITH. I don't believe you.

GREG. Fucking the starfuckers is one of the benefits. But fucking me isn't fucking Lila. Don't get us confused. It's sort of cruel.

KEITH. I'm not confused. I like touching you.

GREG. This is crazy.

KEITH. Tonight is this huge success for you. Maybe I take you out for some food? Talk?

GREG. Well there was this after-party soiree thing –

KEITH. Right.

GREG. – But when you roll your eyes and make cutting remarks to people, friends, all night, the cool kids usually close rank. I don't know what's wrong with me. Eventually, everyone just focused on staring at the walls and writing checks. I sat over in that corner, with a stack of cocktail napkins. Even the interns avoided me.

KEITH. I'm not.

*(**GREG** pulls the tapes out.)*

GREG. It all looks so simple to you, doesn't it?

*(Hands them to **KEITH**.)*

Here. Leak them to your bloggers, post them yourself. Do whatever you want with them.

KEITH. What are these?

GREG. Don't you see the handwriting on the label? These are Lila's new songs.

KEITH. *(Clutches them.) New* songs?

GREG. You came all this way from Missouri –

KEITH. Will you listen to them with me?

GREG. She didn't write them for me, she wrote them for you. All of her fans –

KEITH. If you'll sit down with me and have a conversation –

GREG. *She's* what you came for, so here they are. Take them away from me.

KEITH. Away?

GREG. Sure. This nonsense started when you tapped me on the shoulder in that club, it should end here with you too.

KEITH. I won't if it means you'll never see me again.

GREG. You do know how she died, right? Not the fable spun out in the papers and on TV, but the real way your songstress died?

KEITH. Her heart stopped.

GREG. Right.

KEITH. It's true. My friends were up there, they blogged about watching her being wheeled out on a gurney –

GREG. Blogging is not a substitute for being there.

KEITH. Sometimes she had trouble breathing. It's why she cut back on touring, to just the summer festivals.

GREG. She knew she was over, that younger artists were climbing over her, onto her back, and she didn't care about anyone else. Only herself! So she got this white belt and she went upstairs.

KEITH. There wasn't any blood.

GREG. What?

KEITH. The sheet covering her on the gurney. It was clean. Your sister told us her heart stopped. Lila wouldn't have hurt herself.

GREG. Because you all knew her so well and loved her so much –

KEITH. I saw a photograph. Online, but it was real. Like all of these are real. You weren't there either, Greg. You didn't hold her hand or try to comfort her. I'll bet she liked being alone. Like you do.

GREG. Like –

KEITH. So whatever you think you know –

GREG. I know plenty.

KEITH. – It's not much different than the bloggers. We're all outside, especially now.

GREG. I – I was – I AM her son!

KEITH. Maybe that's why she gave you her new songs. To make up for it. I don't know. I listened to her album on repeat for the entire twenty-three hour bus ride to New York. I didn't talk to anybody the whole way. I'm done with listening by myself.

(Holds out the tapes.)

These are your songs, Greg.

GREG. It's not my job to sell CDs.

KEITH. No, your job is to protect your family. Are you going to do that?

(GREG *takes the tapes back. Pause.)*

GREG. So now what?

KEITH. We walk. My friend works at a bistro nearby. She'll hook us up with some burgers. Then we'll talk. In chairs. At a table. Pepper mill nearby. See what happens.

GREG. I don't know how to do that.

KEITH. Me neither. But it sounds nice.

(Heads for the door.)

So let's try nice.

(GREG *follows* **KEITH.** *Lights change.)*

(Interlude: **MOLLY.***)*

(An ear-splitting, electric guitar screeching version of the song, with groan-like singing.)

(A pool of light finds **MOLLY,** *applying dark makeup to her face, prepping for a show.)*

MOLLY. She came to see my band play once, in a long coat and this wide straw hat with a feather stuck in it, trying to blend in. We had an old musician friend sitting in with us that night, he wrote one of the songs she covered during her old sets. He said we should do that song, since she was there and he was there and why not? And I was a good sport about it, I said, "Sure. It's a thrill to sing with Lila Cante onstage." So the place is packed, people are standing in the windows trying to get a better view, and they're singing along to my words. I felt in my body, knowing this is where I should be. And we get to that moment in our show, and our friend calls her up. Off goes the hat, the coat is thrown behind the drum kit, and I'm saying hello to her tits flopping all over the place, and she brings down the house. Singing the one song that night that wasn't mine.

(Pause.)

MOLLY. Afterward, this photographer guy from *Rolling Stone* shows up and he wants a picture of the three of us. I smile with my teeth, like a ventriloquist dummy. I'm feeling worthy. When the issue comes out, Tracy buys it and finds the page with the "Random Whatevers" on it. The photo's right there, and I'm cropped out of it. Teaches me, smiling on the end. They cut me out of my own backstage photo. So I climb into the back of a crummy van and hit the road, while she slides back into her aloofness, point proven.

(Lights change.)

Scene Three

(One month later. Daytime. The gallery is emptying out. Photographs are wrapped in paper and leaning against the walls in stacks. There is an empty space where **KEITH***'s photograph used to be.)*

*(***GREG*** enters carrying another wrapped frame to find* **NINA** *there, setting up in front of a laptop computer with speakers and headphones.)*

NINA. I've been collecting stories about you.

GREG. I'll bet.

NINA. Every magazine I open –

GREG. It was two interviews.

NINA. But those reviews in the *Times? Newsweek?* Even my Aunt Dottie in Nashville reads *Newsweek.* You're everywhere, Greg.

GREG. It's been an exciting month.

NINA. Your publicist must be a fireball of energy.

GREG. He reminds me of you, actually.

NINA. I meant to put in some face time, but the night I came down there was a line out the door.

GREG. It's been wild. I sold every single print. Parsons students were grabbing postcards last night to hang on their walls.

NINA. Lila would be very proud of you.

GREG. I suppose she would. Look, we're closing up today.

NINA. I see that.

GREG. And there's lots of payment processing to do, so –

NINA. Then I'm glad I caught you. I have the new version of the album with me.

GREG. Right, yes.

*(***GREG*** sets down the wrapped frame.)*

NINA. I told them that the family had to have the first listen before they started pressing CDs.

(Clicking on the computer.)

We re-mastered the bonus tracks and I have the artwork mock-up and a digital version of the booklet.

GREG. How are the essays?

NINA. Kim Deal's a pretty blunt prose writer, but I think she makes Lila seem very influential, very indie.

GREG. Look, my interns just went for coffee –

NINA. Cute fellows. I think they were fellows, I wasn't real sure. I gave them some extra on the street to split a bunt cake.

GREG. I don't have them all day, Nina.

NINA. And we really can't delay this, Greg. Sorry. I need your input and sign-off today. Well, less of your input. More of your signatures!

> *(***NINA*** *pulls out a thick contract, handing it to him.)*

GREG. This is thicker than a novel.

NINA. Saves me from bothering you again.

GREG. Who else has heard this?

NINA. Just my team.

GREG. But you talked to Molly, right?

NINA. She's on the road, isn't she?

GREG. Her band's playing Cake Shop tonight.

NINA. She's in town?

GREG. Uh-huh.

NINA. And playing Cake Shop

> *(Shakes head.)*

Maybe you should loan her your publicist.

> *(Pause.)*

GREG. I'll bet she would swing by so we could do this together.

NINA. Ok, I'm almost set here.

GREG. I can call her.

NINA. So call her. First track is ready to go.

GREG. I'd feel better if my sister were here.

NINA. Molly will throw this computer out the window and I'll have to bill you both for the damage. You are a man of action, Greg. Deal with me. Don't you have photographs to ship and profits to collect?

(**GREG** *sits in front of the computer.*)

GREG. Just set me up for the bonus tracks. I've heard that album enough.

NINA. But the re-mastered sound, Greg.

GREG. (*Puts on the headphones.*) I'll take your word for it.

NINA. Right.

(*Clicks for him.*)

We're calling these "crystalline-sounding postcards from the past" in the press release. Here she is!

(**GREG** *listens.*)

Lila sounds like she's singing in the next room. I can see her sitting in the recording studio, squeezing my hand while she redid her vocals again, then again. Always trying to make them better. Throwing her long hair around and just letting it tangle around the mic. I always had short hair, but I wanted to grow mine out when I saw hers. I can feel her fingers entwined with mine, demanding another take. She could sing forever. Now she will.

(**GREG** *takes off the headphones.*)

GREG. It's you.

NINA. I know it is.

GREG. She screws up the intro and someone laughs. It's you. You're singing with my mother.

NINA. I didn't know she recorded her practices, I thought we were fooling around –

GREG. You said she recorded everything and sent it to you.

NINA. But these were just demos, they didn't mean anything at the time. But now –

GREG. You sound like a frog fucking a kazoo.

NINA. She asked me to sing with her.

GREG. Why would you release that?

NINA. These were in the vault. She wanted me to find them.

GREG. She sang with other musicians.

NINA. I knew the songs.

GREG. At least they made her sound better, not worse.

NINA. Can you hear how passionate we sound together?

GREG. She always sang like that.

NINA. That tenderly?

GREG. That full-throttle.

NINA. Clearly she heard a quality in my voice that inspired her. *We made these.* These are her choices as much as mine!

(**GREG** *is clicking again on the screen.*)

GREG. Are you on every track?

NINA. This is starting to feel personal, Greg.

GREG. Are you singing on every bonus track, Nina?

NINA. She's solo on the last one. She plays final notes on the album alone.

GREG. You're the executive, Nina! Not the artist.

(*Clicking again.*)

Let me see the credits.

NINA. I don't feel comfortable sharing these anymore with you.

GREG. (*Tosses her the contract.*) I'm not signing anything without seeing the credits and my artwork. What else did you change?

NINA. (*Trying to close the computer screen.*) Maybe this can wait until after you've closed your show.

GREG. Where's the cover? Where is my album cover, Nina?

NINA. We, *they*, they decided to go in a new direction for the re-release, distinguish it from the original.

GREG. She picked my photograph for her cover.

>   *(Clicks again.)*

There are three different covers here.

NINA. Fans will buy it for the different covers.

GREG. Nobody is that stupid.

NINA. Each one represents a different side of Lila. Think collector's editions.

GREG. I think I just saw a visual of the frog fucking the kazoo.

NINA. Your cover looks like some communal living ad in a health food magazine. Who gives a fuck about a pair of hands and a ribbon?

GREG. Lila's hands.

>   *(NINA closes the laptop and tosses him back the contract.)*

NINA. Look, you don't have a choice. It's your turn, Greg. I invested money in you.

GREG. You donated to the foundation that funds the gallery.

NINA. Yeah, that's an investment.

GREG. I've already earned that money back.

NINA. I wish you'd believe in me as much as I believed in you. We're both a kind of artist.

GREG. If you think what you and your "team" are churning out is in any way artistically equivalent to what I do, or what my sister tries to do –

NINA. What about the boy, Greg?

GREG. Are you serious?!

NINA. I will track him down.

GREG. You lied. You've always lied about everything.

>   *(MOLLY has entered, guitar-strapped.)*

MOLLY. What your sister "tries" to do. It smells like money in here.

GREG. You've no idea.

MOLLY. Maybe it's Nina.

NINA. Hello Molly! Cake Shop tonight?

MOLLY. Wow, if you're coming it must really be sold out.

NINA. Oh, I'm not coming.

(Turns back to **GREG.***)*

I think we're done here.

MOLLY. What am I interrupting?

NINA. Nothing.

MOLLY. You need one of us, Nina. Her lawyers back me up. We have to authorize Lila Cante calendars if you want them.

GREG. Good, will you deal with her?

MOLLY. You're in the room too, Greg.

NINA. I realize this may be awkward –

MOLLY. Why would that be, Nina?

NINA. Emotionally. I get that.

MOLLY. Why, because Lila killed herself?

NINA. Excuse me – ?

GREG. Molly.

NINA. What did you just say?

MOLLY. Tell her, Greg.

GREG. Molly, don't share this with her. She doesn't deserve –

MOLLY. Say it out loud.

GREG. Lila hung herself upstate. It wasn't a heart attack.

NINA. I – I – N-n-n-n-NO!

MOLLY. And I'm confused. I thought you and Lila were so close.

NINA. WE WERE! She wouldn't have done – *that* – without talking to me!

(Pause.)

GREG. I think Lila did a lot without talking to you.

NINA. So you both knew this?

GREG. I –

MOLLY. Yes. I found her and called Greg immediately.

NINA. And you didn't call me?

MOLLY. Why?

GREG. Why would we do that, Nina?

NINA. We SPOKE! Why is that so difficult for you to believe? She was lonely up there, and she would just call the office. We would have lunch together over the phone. She must have mentioned me.

MOLLY. No.

GREG. Not once.

NINA. Well, I did. I spoke to her that day.

MOLLY. So you knew there were new songs, Nina.

NINA. No.

MOLLY. That's all she talked about.

NINA. I thought she was teasing me –

GREG. Why didn't you believe her?

MOLLY. You've been waiting for a new album.

NINA. She was telling me what I wanted to hear.

GREG. Did you laugh at her?

NINA. No!

MOLLY. Did you make fun of her excitement?

NINA. Of course I didn't.

MOLLY. She liked those summer shows because she could actually see the fans she was singing to, out in the open.

GREG. Instead of a gulf of blackness.

NINA. I didn't know she'd kill herself because of what I said.

MOLLY. No, Nina.

GREG. It had nothing to do with you.

MOLLY. It didn't. It just, it happened.

NINA. She made promises all the time. That she would quit sleeping with guys who stole from her, that she would stop taking so many drugs.

MOLLY. She wasn't on anything. She was clean.

NINA. So why would she do that to herself?

MOLLY. She left us the songs. Right, Greg?

NINA. She would have sent them to me, to my office. We had a routine!

MOLLY. Greg? *Please.*

(**GREG** *pulls out the tapes.*)

GREG. Her handwriting, labeled that day. She made them in the garden upstate with Molly by her side.

(**NINA** *snatches them, scrutinizing.*)

NINA. Yes. There's her handwriting.

MOLLY. I think we're ready to negotiate now.

GREG. Both of us.

MOLLY. One voice.

NINA. I was her friend, your *family's* friend.

MOLLY. So what did you say, when she told you she was writing new songs?

GREG. How were you her friend that day?

NINA. I said, "I'll believe it when I see it, Lila."

MOLLY. So she rushed me to sing these new songs. And to record them. So you could include them on the re-release. You were always part of the plan, Nina.

NINA. I was?

GREG. Instead of those scratchy demos you played me.

MOLLY. Right. She hated those old demos.

NINA. She did?

MOLLY. Her guitar was off-key and she thought she sounded nasally.

NINA. Did she ever mention the other voice, on the harmonies?

MOLLY. No. Why?

NINA. No reason.

    (Pause.)

I think that given the timing and the money we've already spent, maybe it would be better to hold off on setting the final tracklist. Until I get a chance to listen to these.

MOLLY. And you will keep the original cover.

NINA. We have nothing more to say, do we?

GREG. Keep the Kim Deal essay.

NINA. Right.

GREG. It's a smart idea.

NINA. I was full of smart ideas. Uh, I should go. Greg here has legions of collectors waiting on the gift of his art.

GREG. Thanks Nina.

NINA. I hope your interns enjoyed their cake.

    (Turns to MOLLY.*)*

Do they still have guest lists at places like Cake Shop?

MOLLY. I'll see what I can do.

NINA. You know, the two of you, together like this, are a real force. I have a feeling my years of managing Lila's craziness are going to be up to the challenge.

MOLLY. Now we have to create in her shadow, Nina.

NINA. Oh Molly. Some of us live in her shadow.

MOLLY. Wait until her fans hear those songs. You'll be their queen.

    *(*GREG *picks up the contract.)*

GREG. And you won't need my autograph for this.

    *(*NINA *takes it, laughs.)*

NINA. You know what bugs me? Nobody has to try anymore to find good music. They just click a button and it pops up on their computer. There's no work involved, no community to rely on. When I was starting out, knowing about certain bands was like a secret club. The pricks grabbing music – they don't buy it, they grab it – don't need people like me. And it's gonna feel like a fucking shame one day.

> (**NINA** *exits.* **MOLLY** *pulls out another set of tapes.*)

MOLLY. Here you go.

GREG. Where did you get these?

MOLLY. Morris sent me a copy of the copy he made when I got back to Iowa after the funeral. He's always looking out for me.

GREG. Why didn't you just send those to Nina?

MOLLY. I wanted to see what you would do.

GREG. Even Keith doesn't want them. Her devoted fan.

MOLLY. Man, Greg. You can be so stupid sometimes.

> (*Pause.*)

We recorded those songs for you.

> (**MOLLY** *exits.* **GREG** *picks up the tapes and goes over to the stereo, pushing wrapped photographs out of the way.*)
>
> (*He plugs in the headphones, inserts a tape, presses play, and listens. Lights change.*)

Scene Four

(Later that night. Backstage at Cake Shop.)

*(**MOLLY** is tuning her guitar and warming up, sitting on a filthy couch behind a concrete wall. We hear a small crowd gathering outside.)*

*(A curtain pulls back and **GREG** enters with his camera.)*

GREG. Guy running the merch table acts like he was going to slit my throat when I asked where you were.

MOLLY. He's cranky. We stow him under the bus with the amps at night.

GREG. The drummer from the other band came over. He said he had played with Lila at some festival and knew who I was.

MOLLY. Yeah, his band won't be opening for long. Rite Aid is co-sponsoring their next tour.

GREG. He asked if I still took publicity photos.

MOLLY. You would show up at my show and turn it into a career move. I'm about to go onstage, Greg. This is *my* time.

GREG. I can wait outside.

MOLLY. No, what do you want?

GREG. How long are you in town this time?

MOLLY. I'm back to Morris tomorrow night. We're going to make a record in Iowa City this winter. More folky. Trying a new direction.

GREG. Good for you.

MOLLY. Yeah.

GREG. I mean it.

MOLLY. And what exotic wonderland are you off to?

GREG. Chicago.

(Pause.)

But I thought I'd stop in Iowa first. Maybe spend some time. Meet Morris. See the farm.

MOLLY. My life.

GREG. Maybe.

MOLLY. My website has my life. They're called tour dates. Meet up with us in New Orleans if you want to see me.

GREG. I'd rather go to Iowa.

MOLLY. Distance works for us, Greg.

GREG. Molly, I'm sorry.

MOLLY. You're acting like I'm angry, but this isn't anger. I accept you for who you are.

GREG. Who's that?

MOLLY. A brother who doesn't follow me to Iowa.

    (Sets down the guitar.)

I promised Morris we would build a haven in Iowa. He stays there because it insulates him from all of this mess, all that crazy. So I get it.

GREG. You're not like Lila.

MOLLY. You've taught me a lot Greg. I see how easy it is to detach.

GREG. I'm here, aren't I?

MOLLY. Yes. Enjoy the show.

    (She turns away, back to the mirror.)

GREG. That's what she says on the first track. Sit back and enjoy the show. I heard her.

MOLLY. Good.

GREG. And you. There are just as many stories about us as there are songs. She tells that doozy about trying to find new guitar strings in Venice at three in the morning before the bus was scheduled to leave, while that sound guy was teaching me Italian.

MOLLY. The hayride in Nevada.

GREG. We were always with her. It's like my own private concert. Asking me if it's okay to play this song or that, like I'm sitting in front of her. The dirty limerick her grandfather taught her.

MOLLY. She said it made me blush.

GREG. And her singing was so – I know what her fans get so excited about! It's like I'm listening with them. Then she plays this song that I know, that I'm sitting there wondering how I could know this brand-new song she just wrote.

MOLLY. She had been writing for a while.

GREG. And then I realized it was our song!

MOLLY. Your song.

GREG. We wrote this song together, before I left home. She reworked the music and changed the tempo, but she kept my words. Ten years and she didn't change our words. Just silly words, but it was nice to hear.

MOLLY. Touring is about the only way I make any money, but the reason I still get up on stages like that crummy box out there is so I can feel a little less like her daughter and more like myself. It's just me up there. Funny, though, when we were singing together again, out in the garden, for you, I didn't mind being her daughter. I felt so lucky sitting there. I look for her out there now.

GREG. She sings the last line and then whispers "That's it."

MOLLY. She went into the house and up the stairs.

(*Pause.*)

GREG. I worked so hard to get here.

MOLLY. Choices.

GREG. Throwing a camera in a bag and bolting, just to get away from her.

MOLLY. Easy.

GREG. Now I'm not so sure. I'm sorry I left you behind, Molly.

(*There is a loud banging on the door.* **MOLLY** *grabs her guitar.*)

MOLLY. I'm adding your song into the show tonight. You better be ready to get up onstage.

GREG. Oh I'm not going onstage.

MOLLY. Man, you spent your diaper years on a stage. We'll do it as the first encore.

GREG. But nobody's going to know it yet.

MOLLY. But we're not going to do it Lila's way. We're going to blues it up, make it our own.

GREG. I don't "blues it up."

(**MOLLY** *starts the intro on her guitar.*)

MOLLY. Follow me. C'mon.

GREG. Where are the words?

MOLLY. You wrote them! Are you ready?

GREG. Whoa. I just got nervous.

MOLLY. It's called adrenaline, brother. Okay, here we go!

(*Begins singing the song, the same song we've heard throughout the play in its different forms.*)

YOU COULD TRY THE TRAPEZE
YOU COULD BUILD A FORT IN YOUR YARD
YOU COULD WRITE THE SAD SONGS
YOU COULD TRY SOMETHING HARD

(**GREG** *joins her, tentative at first.*)

GREG/MOLLY.

I COULD BE A MODEL

MOLLY.

I COULD START A WAR WITH YOUR HEART

GREG/MOLLY.

I COULD WORK AT ONE THING
WHILE YOU FALL APART

(**BOTH** *stare at each other.*)

MOLLY. Nice.

(*Sings.*)

YOU COULD BUILD A GREENHOUSE

GREG. *(Echoes her.)*

YOU COULD BUILD A GREENHOUSE

MOLLY.

YOU COULD MAKE A WORLD OF YOUR OWN

GREG.

YOU COULD MAKE A WORLD OF YOUR OWN

MOLLY.

YOU COULD MAKE IT MAGIC

GREG.

YOU COULD MAKE IT MAGIC

MOLLY.

AND ALL THE FLOWERS WOULD GROW

> *(They are singing together now, full-voiced and in perfect harmony.)*

GREG.

I COULD BE A SAVIOR

STILL CRUSH WHAT BLOOMS IN YOUR HEART

MOLLY.

OH I COULD HIT ROCK BOTTOM

GREG. *(Echo.)*

I COULD HIT ROCK BOTTOM

MOLLY.

YEAH

GREG/MOLLY.

WHILE YOU FALL APART

> *(**MOLLY** lets loose, **GREG** raptly watching her.)*

MOLLY.

BUT MY HEART SAYS

MORE OF THE SAME, YEAH,

MORE OF THE SAME

DON'T I WISH IT WERE

MORE OF THE SAME TOUCH, SAME SIGHT

SAME BRIGHT FLAME IN THE DIRT

BRIGHT AS THE FLAME, YEAH,

MORE OF THE SAME, YEAH

BUT YOU'RE NOT HERE CALLING MY –

NOT HERE CALLING MY NAME –

*(**GREG** takes her photo.)*

GREG. That's it.

MOLLY. Ha. You finally got me.

(The noise from the crowd outside grows. The band is about to take the stage.)

End of Play

More Of The Same

6/21/16

I could work at___ one thing___ while you fall___ a - part___

C#m   B   G#m

F#m   /A   B2   F#m   /A   B/C#   F#m

You could build a green-house   You could make a world of your own

You could build a green-house

F#m   /A   B2   F#m   /A   B2

You could make it ma - gic   And all the flow-ers would grow   And

flow - ers

F#m   /A   B2   F#m   /A   B2